ROYAL BOROUGH OF GREENWICH

Tony Ross is one of the most popular and successful
of all children's illustrators, with almost 50 picture books
to his name. He has also produced line drawings for
many fiction titles, for authors such as David Walliams,
Enid Blyton, Astrid Lindgren and many more.

For a complete list of **Horrid Henry** titles
see the end of the book, or visit
www.horridhenry.co.uk
or
www.hachettechildrens.co.uk

HORRiD HENRY
School's Out

Francesca Simon
Illustrated by Tony Ross

Orion
Children's Books

ORION CHILDREN'S BOOKS
This collection first published in Great Britain in 2018
by Hodder and Stoughton
1 3 5 7 9 10 8 6 4 2

A CIP catalogue record for this book
is available from the British Library.

ISBN 978 1 5101 0516 4

Printed and bound in Great Britain by Clays Ltd, St Ives plc

The paper and board used in this book are from
well-managed forests and other responsible sources.

An Hachette UK Company
www.hachette.co.uk
www.hachettechildrens.co.uk
www.horridhenry.co.uk

CONTENTS

HORRiD HENRY AND THE SECRET CLUB

'Halt! Who goes there?'

'Me.'

'Who's me?' said Moody
Margaret.

'ME!' said Sour Susan.

'What's the password?'

'Uhhhh . . .' Sour Susan paused. What
was the password? She thought and
thought and thought.

'Potatoes?'

Margaret sighed loudly. Why was

she friends with such a stupid person?

'No it isn't.'

'Yes it is,' said Susan.

'Potatoes was last week's password,' said Margaret.

'No it wasn't.'

'Yes it was,' said Moody Margaret. 'It's my club and I decide.'

There was a long pause.

'All right,' said Susan sourly. 'What *is* the password?'

'I don't know if I'm going to tell you,' said Margaret. 'I could be giving away a big secret to the enemy.'

'But I'm not the enemy,' said Susan. 'I'm Susan.'

'Shhhh!' said Margaret. 'We don't want Henry to find out who's in the secret club.'

Susan looked quickly over her shoulder.

The enemy 'was nowhere
to be seen'. She whistled twice.

'All clear,' said Sour Susan.
'Now let me in.'

Moody Margaret thought for a
moment. Letting someone in without
the password broke the first club rule.

'Prove to me you're Susan, and not
the enemy pretending to be Susan,'
said Margaret.

'You know it's me,' wailed Susan.

'Prove it.'

Susan stuck her foot into the tent.

'I'm wearing the black patent
leather shoes with the blue flowers
I always wear.'

'No good,' said Margaret. 'The
enemy could have stolen them.'

'I'm speaking with Susan's voice
and I look like Susan,' said Susan.

3

'No good,' said Margaret. 'The enemy could be a master of disguise.'

Susan stamped her foot. 'And I know that you were the one who pinched Helen and I'm going to tell Miss . . .'

'Come closer to the tent flap,' said Margaret.

Susan bent over.

'Now listen to me,' said Margaret. 'Because I'm only going to tell you once. When a secret club member wants to come in they say "NUNGA." Anyone inside answers back, "Nunga Nu." That's how I know it's you and you know it's me.

'Nunga,' said Sour Susan.

'Nunga Nu,' said Moody Margaret. 'Enter.'

Susan entered the club. She gave the secret handshake, sat down on her box and sulked.

'You knew it was me all along,' said Susan.

Margaret scowled at her.

'That's not the point. If you don't want to obey the club rules you can leave.'

Susan didn't move.

'Can I have a biscuit?' she said. Margaret smiled graciously. 'Have two,' she said. 'Then we'll get down to business.'

Meanwhile, hidden under a bush behind some strategically placed branches, another top secret meeting was taking place in the next door garden.

'I think that's everything,' said the Leader. 'I shall now put the plans into action.'

'What am I going to do?' said Perfect Peter.

'Stand guard,' said Horrid Henry. 'I always have to stand guard,' said Peter, as the Leader crept out.

'It's not fair.'

★

'Have you brought your spy report?'
asked Margaret.

'Yes,' said Susan.

'Read it aloud,' said Margaret.

Susan took out a piece of paper and
read:

'I watched the enemy's house for two
hours yesterday morning—'

'Which morning?' interrupted
Margaret.

'Saturday morning,' said Susan.
'A lady with grey hair and a beret
walked past.'

'What colour was the beret?' said
Margaret.

'I don't know,' said Susan.

'Call yourself a spy and you don't
know what colour the beret was,'
said Margaret.

'Can I please continue with my
report?' said Susan.

'I'm not stopping you,' said Margaret.

'Then I saw the enemy leave the
house with his brother and mother. The
enemy kicked his brother twice. His
mother shouted at him. Then I
saw the postman—'

'NUNGA!' screeched a voice from
outside.

Margaret and Susan froze.

'NUNGA!!!'

8

screeched the voice again. 'I know you're in there!'

'Aaaahh!' squeaked Susan. 'It's Henry!'

'Quick! Hide!' hissed Margaret.

The secret spies crouched behind two boxes.

'You told him our password!' hissed Margaret. 'How dare you!'

'Wasn't me!' hissed Susan. 'I couldn't even remember it, so how could I have told him? You told him!'

'Didn't,' hissed Margaret.

'NUNGA!!!' screeched Henry again. 'You have to let me in! I know the password.'

'What do we do?' hissed Susan. 'You said anyone who knows the password enters.'

'For the last time, NUNGAAAAA!' shouted Horrid Henry.

'Nunga Nu,' said Margaret.
'Enter.'

Henry swaggered into the tent. Margaret glared at him.

'Don't mind if I do,' said Henry, grabbing all the chocolate biscuits and stuffing them into his mouth. Then he sprawled on the rug, scattering crumbs everywhere.

'What are you doing?' said Horrid Henry.

'Nothing,' said Moody Margaret.

'Nothing,' said Sour Susan.

'You are, too,' said Henry.

'Mind your own business,' said Margaret. 'Now, Susan, let's vote on whether to allow boys in. I vote No.'

'I vote No, too,' said Susan. 'Sorry, Henry, you can't join. Now leave.'

'No,' said Henry.

'LEAVE,' said Margaret.

'Make me,' said Henry.

Margaret took a deep breath. Then she opened her mouth and screamed. No one could scream as loud, or as long, or as piercingly, as Moody Margaret. After a few moments, Susan started screaming too.

Henry got to his feet, knocking
over the crate they used as a table.

'Watch out,' said Henry.
'Because the Purple Hand will be back!'
He turned to go.

Moody Margaret sprang up behind
him and pushed him through the flap.
Henry landed in a heap outside.

'Can't get me!' shouted Henry.
He picked himself up and jumped
over the wall. 'The Purple Hand is
the best!'

'Oh yeah,' muttered Margaret. 'We'll
see about that.'

Henry checked over his shoulder to
make sure no one was watching. Then
he crept back to his fort.

'Smelly toads,' he whispered to
the guard.

The branches parted. Henry

climbed in.

'Did you attack them?' said Peter.

'Of course,' said Henry. 'Didn't you hear Margaret screaming?'

'I was the one who heard their password, so I think I should have gone,' said Peter.

'Whose club is this?' said Henry.

The corners of Peter's mouth began to turn down.

'Right, out!' said Henry.

'Sorry!' said Peter. 'Please, Henry, can I be a real member of the Purple Hand?'

'No,' said Henry. 'You're too young. And don't you dare come into the fort when I'm not here.'

'I won't,' said Peter.

'Good,' said Henry. 'Now here's the plan. I'm going to set a booby trap in Margaret's tent. Then when she goes in . . .' Henry shrieked with

laughter as he pictured Moody
Margaret covered in cold muddy
water.

All was not well back at Moody
Margaret's Secret Club.

'It's your fault,' said Margaret.

'It isn't,' said Susan.

'You're such a blabbermouth, and
you're a terrible spy.'

'I am not,' said Susan.

'Well, I'm Leader, and I ban you
from the club for a week for breaking
our sacred rule and telling the enemy
our password. Now go away.'

'Oh please let me stay,' said
Susan.

'No,' said Margaret.

Susan knew there was no point
arguing with Margaret when she got

that horrible bossy look on her face.

'You're so mean,' said Susan.

Moody Margaret picked up a book and started to read.

Sour Susan got up and left.

'I know what I'll do to fix Henry,' thought Margaret. 'I'll set a booby trap in Henry's fort. Then when he goes in . . .' Margaret shrieked with laughter as she pictured Horrid Henry covered in cold muddy water.

Just before lunch Henry sneaked into Margaret's garden holding a plastic bucket of water and some string. He stretched the string just above the ground across the entrance and suspended the bucket above, with the other end of the string tied round it.

15

Just after lunch Margaret sneaked into
Henry's garden holding a bucket of
water and some string. She stretched
the string across the fort's entrance
and rigged up the bucket. What she
wouldn't give to see Henry soaking
wet when he tripped over the string
and pulled the bucket of water down
on him.

Perfect Peter came into the garden
carrying a ball. Henry wouldn't play
with him and there was nothing to
do.

Why shouldn't I go into the fort?
thought Peter. I helped build it.

Next door, Sour Susan slipped into
the garden. She was feeling sulky.

Why shouldn't I go into the tent?
thought Susan. It's my club too.

Perfect Peter walked into the fort
and tripped.

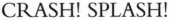
CRASH! SPLASH!

Sour Susan walked into the tent and tripped.

CRASH! SPLASH!

Horrid Henry heard howls. He ran into the garden whooping.

'Ha! Ha! Margaret! Gotcha!'

Then he stopped.

Moody Margaret heard screams. She ran into the garden cheering.

'Ha! Ha! Henry! Gotcha!'

Then she stopped.

'That's it!' shrieked Peter. 'I'm leaving!'

'But it wasn't me,' said Henry.

'That's it!' sobbed Susan. 'I quit!'

'But it wasn't me,' said Margaret.

'Rats!' said Henry.

'Rats!' said Margaret.

They glared at each other.

Henry's Summer Howlers

Why did the crab
go to jail?
He kept pinching
things.

Where do cows go on holiday?
Moo Zealand.

Why did the egg go into
the jungle?
*Because it was an
EGG-splorer.*

Why are bananas so good
at gymnastics?
They are great at doing the splits.

Henry's Summer Howlers

What do you call a camel
with three lumps?
Lumpy.

Why did Miss Battle-Axe
jump in the pool?
*She wanted to test
the water.*

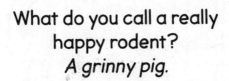

What do you call a really
happy rodent?
A grinny pig.

What do you call an
exploding monkey?
A Baboom.

HORRID HENRY AND THE MEGA-MEAN TIME MACHINE

Horrid Henry flicked the switch. The time machine whirred. Dials spun. Buttons pulsed. Latches locked. Horrid Henry Time Traveller was ready for blast off!

Now, where to go, where to go?

Dinosaurs, thought Henry. Yes! Henry loved dinosaurs. He would love to stalk a few Tyrannosaurus Rexes as they rampaged through the primordial jungle.

But what about King Arthur and the

Knights of the Round Table? 'Arise,
Sir Henry,' King Arthur would say,
booting Lancelot out of his chair.
'Sure thing, King,' Sir Henry would
reply, twirling his sword. 'Out of my
way, worms!'

Or what about the siege of Troy?
Heroic Henry, that's who he'd be, the
fearless fighter dashing about doing
daring deeds.

Tempting, thought Henry. Very
tempting.

Wait a sec, what about visiting the
future, where school was banned and
parents had to do whatever their
children told them? Where everyone
had their own spaceship and ate sweets
for dinner. And where King Henry the
Horrible ruled supreme, chopping off
the head of anyone who dared to say
no to him.

To the future, thought Henry, setting the dial.

Bang! Pow!

Henry braced himself for the jolt into hyperspace – 10, 9, 8, 7, 6 –

'Henry, it's my turn.'

Horrid Henry ignored the alien's whine.

– 5, 4, 3 –

'Henry! If you don't share I'm going to tell Mum.'

AAAARRRRGGGHHHHHH. The Time Machine juddered to a halt. Henry climbed out.

'Go away, Peter,' said Henry. 'You're spoiling everything.'

'But it's my turn.'

'GO AWAY!'

'Mum said we could *both* play with the box,' said Peter. 'We could cut out windows, make a little house, paint flowers— '

'NO!' screeched Henry.

'But . . . ' said Peter. He stood in the sitting room, holding his scissors and crayons.

'Don't you touch my box!' hissed Henry.

'I will if I want to,' said Peter. 'And it's not yours.' Henry had no right to boss him around, thought Peter. He'd been waiting such a long time for his turn. Well, he wasn't waiting any longer. He'd start cutting out a window this minute.

Peter got out his scissors.

'Stop! It's a time machine, you toad!' shrieked Henry.

Peter paused.

Peter gasped.

Peter stared at the huge cardboard box. A time machine? *A time machine?* How could it be a time machine?

'It is not,' said Peter.

'Is too,' said Henry.

'But it's made of cardboard,' said Peter. 'And the washing machine came in it.'

Henry sighed.

'Don't you know anything? If it *looked* like a time machine everyone would try to steal it. It's a time machine in *disguise.*'

Peter looked at the time machine. On the one hand he didn't believe Henry for one minute. This was just one of

Henry's tricks. Peter was a hundred million billion percent certain Henry was lying.

On the other hand, what if Henry *was* telling the truth for once and there was a real time machine in his sitting room?

'If it *is* a time machine I want to have a go,' said Peter.

'You can't. You're too young,' said Henry.

'Am not.'

'Are too.'

Perfect Peter stuck out his bottom lip.

'I don't believe you anyway.'

Horrid Henry was outraged.

'Okay, I'll prove it. I'll go to the future right now. Stand back. Don't move.'

Horrid Henry leapt into the box and closed the lid. The Time Machine began to shudder and shake.

Then everything was still for a very long time.

Perfect Peter didn't know what to do. What if Henry was gone – forever? What if he were stuck in the future?

I could have his room, thought Peter.

I could watch whatever I wanted on telly. I could—

Suddenly the box tipped over and Horrid Henry staggered out.

'Wh-wh- where am I?' he stuttered. Then he collapsed on the floor.

Peter stared at Henry.

Henry stared wildly at Peter.

'I've been to the future!' gasped
Henry, panting. 'It was amazing. Wow.
I met my great-great-great-grandson.
He still lives in this house. And he looks
just like me.'

'So he's ugly,' muttered Peter.

'What – did – you – say?' hissed
Henry.

'Nothing,' said Peter quickly. He
didn't know what to think. 'Is this a
trick, Henry?'

'Course it isn't,' said Henry. 'And just
for that I won't let you have a go.'

'I can if I want to,' said Peter.

'You keep away from my time
machine,' said Henry. 'One wrong
move and you'll get blasted into the
future.'

Perfect Peter walked a few steps

towards the time machine. Then he
paused.

'What's it like in the future?'

'Boys wear dresses,' said Horrid
Henry. 'And lipstick. People talk
Ugg language. *You'd* probably like it.
Everyone just eats vegetables.'

'Really?'

'And kids have loads of homework.'

Perfect Peter loved homework.

'Ooohh.' This Peter *had* to see. Just in case Henry *was* telling the truth.

'I'm going to the future and you can't stop me,' said Peter.

'Go ahead,' said Henry. Then he snorted. 'You can't go looking like that!'

'Why not?' said Peter.

''Cause everyone will laugh at you.'

Perfect Peter hated people laughing at him.

'Why?'

'Because to them you'll look weird. Are you sure you really want to go to the future?'

'Yes,' said Peter.

'Are you sure you're sure?'

'YES,' said Peter.

'Then I'll get you ready,' said Henry solemnly.

'Thank you, Henry,' said Peter.
Maybe he'd been wrong about Henry.
Maybe going to the future had turned
him into a nice brother.

Horrid Henry dashed out of the sitting
room.

Perfect Peter felt a quiver of
excitement. The future. What if Henry
really was telling the truth?

Horrid Henry returned carrying a
large wicker basket. He pulled out an
old red dress of Mum's, some lipstick,
and a black frothy drink.

'Here, put this on,' said Henry.

Perfect Peter put on the dress. It
dragged onto the floor.

'Now, with a bit of lipstick,' said
Horrid Henry, applying big blobs of red
lipstick all over Peter's face, 'you'll fit
right in. Perfect,' he said, standing back
to admire his handiwork. 'You look just

like a boy from the future.'

'Okay,' said Perfect Peter.

'Now listen carefully,' said Henry. 'When you arrive, you won't be able to speak the language unless you drink this bibble babble drink. Take this with you and drink it when you get there.'

Henry held out the frothy black drink from his Dungeon Drink Kit. Peter took it.

'You can now enter the time machine.'

Peter obeyed. His heart was pounding.

'Don't get out until the time machine has stopped moving completely. Then count to twenty-five, and open the hatch very very slowly. You don't want a bit of you in the twenty-third century, and the rest here in the twenty-first. Good luck.'

Henry swirled the box round and round and round. Peter began to feel dizzy. The drink sloshed on the floor.

Then everything was still.

Peter's head was spinning. He counted to twenty-five, then crept out.

He was in the sitting room of a house that looked just like his. A boy wearing a bathrobe and silver waggly antennae with his face painted in blue stripes stood in front of him.

'Ugg?' said the strange boy.

'Henry?' said Peter.

'Uggg uggg bleuch ble bloop,' said the boy.

'Uggg uggg,' said Peter uncertainly.

'Uggh uggh drink ugggh,' said the boy, pointing to Peter's bibble babble drink.

Peter drank the few drops which were left.

'I'm Zog,' said Zog. 'Who are you?'

'I'm Peter,' said Peter.

'Ahhhhh! Welcome! You must be my great-great-great-uncle Peter. Your very nice brother Henry told me all about you when he visited me from the past.'

'Oh, what did he say?' said Peter.

'That you were an ugly toad.'

'I am not,' said Peter. 'Wait a minute,' he added suspiciously. 'Henry said that boys wore dresses in the future.'

'They do,' said Zog quickly. 'I'm a girl.'

'Oh,' said Peter. He gasped. Henry would *never* in a million years say he was a girl. Not even if he were being poked with red hot pokers. Could it be. . .

Peter looked around. 'This looks just like my sitting room.'

Zog snorted.

'Of course it does, Uncle Pete. This is

now the Peter Museum. You're famous in the future. Everything has been kept exactly as it was.'

Peter beamed. He was famous in the future. He always knew he'd be famous. A Peter Museum! He couldn't wait to tell Spotless Sam and Tidy Ted.

There was just one more thing . . .

'What about Henry?' he asked. 'Is he famous too?'

'Nah,' said Zog smoothly. 'He's known as What's-His-Name, Peter's older brother.'

Ahh. Peter swelled with pride. Henry was in his lowly place, at last. That proved it. He'd really travelled to the future!

Peter looked out the window. Strange how the future didn't look so different from his own time.

Zog pointed.

'Our spaceships,' he announced.

Peter stared. Spaceships looked just like cars.

'Why aren't they flying?' said Peter.

'Only at night time,' said Zog. 'You can either drive 'em or fly 'em.'

'Wow,' said Peter.

'Don't *you* have spaceships?' said Zog.

'No,' said Peter. 'Cars.'

'I didn't know they had cars in olden days,' said Zog. 'Do you have blitzkatrons and zappersnappers?'

'No,' said Peter. 'What— '

The front door slammed. Mum
walked in. She stared at Peter.

'What on earth. . .'

'Don't be scared,' said Peter. 'I'm
Peter. I come from the past. I'm your
great-great-great grandfather.'

Mum looked at Peter.

Peter looked at Mum.

'Why are you wearing my dress?' said
Mum.

'It's not one of *yours*, silly,' said Peter.
'It belonged to my mum.'

'I see,' said Mum.

'Come on, Uncle Pete,' said Zog
quickly, taking Peter firmly by the arm,
'I'll show you our supersonic hammock
in the garden.'

'Okay, Zog,' said Peter happily.

Mum beamed.

'It's so lovely to see you playing nicely
with your brother, Henry.'

Perfect Peter stood still.

'What did you call him?'

'Henry,' said Mum.

Peter felt a chill.

'So his name's not Zog? And he's not
a girl?'

'Not the last time I looked,' said
Mum.

'And this house isn't . . . the Peter
Museum?'

Mum glared at Henry. 'Henry! Have
you been teasing Peter again?'

'Ha ha tricked you!' shrieked Henry.

41

'Na Na Ne Nah Nah, wait till I tell everybody!'

'NO!' squealed Peter.

'NOOOOOOO!' How *could* he have believed his horrible brother?

'Henry! You horrid boy! Go to your room! No TV for the rest of the day,' said Mum.

But Horrid Henry didn't care. The Mega-Mean Time Machine would go down in history as his greatest trick ever.

Henry's Summer Howlers

DAD: I hate to say this but your swimming costume is very tight.
MUM: *Wear your own then!*

What do double agents play when they go on holiday?
I spy.

Where do cats go on holiday?
The Canary Islands.

What do you get when you cross a sorceress with a millionaire?
A very witch person.

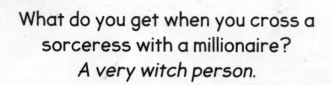

Henry's Summer Howlers

MISS BATTLE AXE: What did you learn during the summer holidays, Henry?
HENRY: *That seven weeks isn't long enough to tidy my bedroom.*

What do you get when you cross a monkey with a flower?
A chimp-pansy.

Have you ever seen a fish cry?
No, but I've seen a whale blubber.

What does a toad say when he sees something he likes?
"That's toad-ally awesome!"

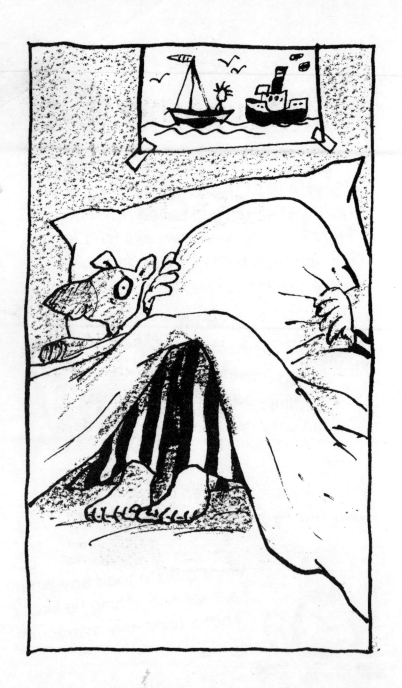

HORRID HENRY AND THE SWIMMING LESSON

Oh no! thought Horrid Henry. He pulled the duvet tightly over his head. It was Thursday. Horrible, horrible, Thursday. The worst day of the week. Horrid Henry was certain Thursdays came more often than any other day.

47

Thursday was his class swimming day.
Henry had a nagging feeling that this
Thursday was even worse than all the
other awful Thursdays. Horrid Henry
liked the bus ride to the pool. Horrid
Henry liked doing the dance of the
seven towels in the changing room.
He also liked hiding in the lockers,

throwing socks in the pool, and
splashing everyone.

The only thing Henry didn't like
about going swimming was . . .
swimming.

The truth was, Horrid Henry hated
water. Ugggh! Water was so . . . wet!
And soggy. The chlorine stung his eyes.
He never knew what horrors might be
lurking in the deep end. And the pool
was so cold penguins could fly in for
the winter.

Fortunately, Henry had a brilliant list
of excuses. He'd pretend he had a
verucca, or a tummy ache, or had lost
his swimming costume. Unfortunately,
the mean, nasty, horrible swimming
teacher, Soggy Sid, usually made him
get in the pool anyway.

Then Henry would duck Dizzy
Dave, or splash Weepy William, or

pinch Gorgeous Gurinder, until Sid
ordered him out. It was not surprising
that Horrid Henry had never managed
to get his five-metre badge.

Arrrgh! Now he remembered.
Today was test day. The terrible day
when everyone had to show how far
they could swim. Aerobic Al was going
for gold. Moody Margaret was going
for silver. The only ones who were
still trying for their five-metre badges
were Lazy Linda and Horrid Henry.
Five whole metres! How could anyone
swim such a vast distance?

If only they were tested on who
could sink to the bottom of the pool the
fastest, or splash the most, or spit water
the furthest, then Horrid Henry would
have every badge in a jiffy. But no. He
had to leap into a freezing cold pool,
and, if he survived that shock, somehow

thrash his way across five whole metres without drowning.

Well, there was no way he was going to school today.

Mum came into his room.

'I can't go to school today, Mum,' Henry moaned. 'I feel terrible.'

Mum didn't even look at him.

'Thursday-itis again, I presume,' said Mum.

'No way!' said Henry. 'I didn't even know it was Thursday.'

'Get up Henry,' said Mum. 'You're going swimming and that's that.'

Perfect Peter peeked round the door.

'It's badge day today!' he said. 'I'm going for 50 metres!'

'That's brilliant, Peter,' said Mum. 'I bet you're the best swimmer in your class.'

Perfect Peter smiled modestly.

'I just try my best,' he said. 'Good
luck with your five-metre badge,
Henry,' he added.

Horrid Henry growled and attacked.
He was a Venus flytrap slowly mashing
a frantic fly between his deadly leaves.

'Eeeeeowwww!' screeched Peter.

'Stop being horrid, Henry!' screamed
Mum. 'Leave your poor brother alone!'

Horrid Henry let Peter go. If only
he could find some way not to take his

swimming test he'd be the happiest boy
in the world.

Henry's class arrived at the pool.
Right, thought Henry. Time to unpack
his excuses to Soggy Sid.

'I can't go swimming, I've got a
verucca,' lied Henry.

'Take off your sock,' ordered Soggy
Sid.

Rats, thought Henry.

'Maybe it's better now,' said Henry.

'I thought so,' said Sid.

Horrid Henry grabbed his stomach.

'Tummy pains!' he moaned. 'I feel
terrible.'

'You seemed fine when you were
prancing round the pool a moment
ago,' snapped Sid. 'Now get changed.'

Time for the killer excuse.

'I forgot my swimming costume!' said

Henry. This was his best chance of success.

'No problem,' said Soggy Sid. He handed Henry a bag. 'Put on one of these.'

Slowly, Horrid Henry rummaged in the bag. He pulled out a bikini top, a blue costume with a hole in the middle, a pair of pink pants, a tiny pair of green trunks, a polka-dot one piece with bunnies, see-through white shorts, and a nappy.

'I can't wear any of these!' protested Horrid Henry.

'You can and you will, if I have to put them on you myself,' snarled Sid.

Horrid Henry squeezed into the green trunks. He could barely breathe. Slowly, he joined the rest of his class pushing and shoving by the side of the pool.

Everyone had millions of badges sewn all over their costumes. You couldn't even see Aerobic Al's bathing suit beneath the stack of badges.

'Hey you!' shouted Soggy Sid. He pointed at Weepy William. 'Where's your swimming costume?'

Weepy William glanced down and burst into tears.

'Waaaaah,' he wailed, and ran weeping back to the changing room.

'Now get in!' ordered Soggy Sid.

'But I'll drown!' screamed Henry.
'I can't swim!'

'Get in!' screamed Soggy Sid.

Goodbye, cruel world. Horrid Henry
held his breath and fell into the icy
water. ARRRRGH! He was turning
into an iceberg!

He was dying! He was dead! His feet
flailed madly as he sank down, down,
down – clunk! Henry's feet touched the
bottom.

Henry stood up, choking and
spluttering. He was waist-deep in water.

'Linda and Henry! Swim five metres –
now!'

What am I going to do? thought
Henry. It was so humiliating not
even being able to swim five metres!
Everyone would tease him. And he'd
have to listen to them bragging about
their badges! Wouldn't it be great to

get a badge? Somehow?

Lazy Linda set off, very very slowly.
Horrid Henry grabbed on to her leg.
Maybe she'll pull me across, he thought.

'Ugggh!' gurgled Lazy Linda.

'Leave her alone!' shouted Sid. 'Last
chance, Henry.'

Horrid Henry ran along the pool's
bottom and flapped his arms, pretending
to swim.

'Did it!' said Henry.

Soggy Sid scowled.

'I said swim, not walk!' screamed Sid. 'You've failed. Now get over to the far lane and practise. Remember, anyone who stops swimming during the test doesn't get a badge.'

Horrid Henry stomped over to the far lane. No way was he going to practise! How he hated swimming! He watched the others splashing up and down, up and down. There was Aerobic Al, doing his laps like a bolt of lightning. And Moody Margaret. And Kung-Fu Kate. Everyone would be getting a badge but

Henry. It was so unfair.

'Pssst, Susan,' said Henry. 'Have you heard? There's a shark in the deep end!'

'Oh yeah, right,' said Sour Susan. She looked at the dark water in the far end of the pool.

'Don't believe me,' said Henry. 'Find out the hard way. Come back with a leg missing.'

Sour Susan paused and whispered something to Moody Margaret.

'Shut up, Henry,' said Margaret. They swam off.

'Don't worry about the shark, Andrew,' said Henry. 'I think he's already eaten today.'

'What shark?' said Anxious Andrew.

Andrew stared at the deep end. It did look awfully dark down there.

'Start swimming, Andrew!' shouted Soggy Sid.

'I don't want to,' said Andrew.

'Swim! Or I'll bite you myself!' snarled Sid.

Andrew started swimming.

'Dave, Ralph, Clare, and Bert – start swimming!' bellowed Soggy Sid.

'Look out for the shark!' said Horrid Henry. He watched Aerobic Al tearing up and down the lane. 'Gotta swim, gotta swim, gotta swim,' muttered Al between strokes.

What a show-off, thought Henry. Wouldn't it be fun to play a trick on him?

Horrid Henry pretended he was a crocodile. He sneaked under the water to the middle of the pool and waited until Aerobic Al swam overhead. Then Horrid Henry reached up.

Pinch! Henry grabbed Al's thrashing leg.

'AAAARGGG!' screamed Al. 'Something's grabbed my leg. Help!' Aerobic Al leaped out of the pool.

Tee hee, thought Horrid Henry.

'It's a shark!' screamed Sour Susan. She scrambled out of the pool.

'There's a shark in the pool!' screeched Anxious Andrew.

'There's a shark in the pool!' howled Rude Ralph.

Everyone was screaming and shouting and struggling to get out.

The only one left in the pool was Henry.

Shark!

Horrid Henry forgot there were no sharks in swimming pools.

Horrid Henry forgot *he'd* started the shark rumour.

Horrid Henry forgot he couldn't swim.

All he knew was that he was alone in the pool – with a shark!

Horrid Henry swam for his life. Shaking and quaking, splashing and crashing, he torpedoed his way to the side of the pool and scrambled out. He gasped and panted. Thank goodness. Safe at last! He'd never ever go swimming again.

'Five metres!' bellowed Soggy Sid. 'You've all failed your badges today, except for – Henry!'

'Waaaaaaahhhhhh!' wailed the other children.

'Whoopee!' screamed Henry. 'Olympics, here I come!'

Henry's Summer Howlers

Why did the golfer wear
two pairs of pants?
*In case he got a hole
in one.*

How can you tell
if a dinosaur is a
vegetarian?
Lie down on a plate.

How does an elephant
get up a tree?
*Sits on an acorn and
waits for it to grow.*

What's an insect's
favourite game?
Cricket.

Henry's Summer Howlers

What part of a swimming
pool is never the same?
The changing rooms.

Mum: Henry, why did you put a
slug in Aunt Ruby's bed?
Henry: *I couldn't find a snake.*

Why was the bee's
hair sticky?
*Because he used a
honey-comb.*

Where do you find giant snails?
On the end of a giant's fingers.

HORRID HENRY
READS A BOOK

Blah blah blah blah blah.

Miss Battle-Axe droned on and on and on. Horrid Henry drew pictures of crocodiles tucking into a juicy Battle-Axe snack in his maths book.

Snap! Off went her head.

Yank! Bye bye leg.

Crunch! Ta-ta teeth.

Yum yum. Henry's crocodile had a big fat smile on its face.

Blah blah blah books blah blah blah read blah blah blah prize blah blah

. . . PRIZE?

Horrid Henry stopped doodling.

'What prize?' he shrieked.

'Don't shout out, Henry,' said Miss Battle-Axe.

Horrid Henry waved his hand and shouted:

'What prize?'

'Well, Henry, if you'd been paying attention instead of scribbling, you'd know, wouldn't you?' said Miss Battle-Axe.

Horrid Henry scowled. Typical teacher. You're interested enough in what they're saying to ask a question, and suddenly they don't want to answer.

'So class, as I was saying before I was so rudely interrupted—' she glared at Horrid Henry—'you'll have two weeks to read as many books as you can for our school reading competition.

Whoever reads the most books will win an exciting prize. A very exciting prize. But remember, a book report on every book on your list, please.'

Oh. A reading competition. Horrid Henry slumped in his chair. Phooey. Reading was hard, heavy work. Just turning the pages made Henry feel exhausted. Why couldn't they ever do fun competitions, like whose tummy could rumble the loudest, or who shouted out the most in class, or who

knew the rudest words? Horrid Henry
would win *those* competitions every
time.

But no. Miss Battle-Axe would
never have a *fun* competition. Well,
no way was he taking part in a reading
contest. Henry would just have to watch
someone undeserving like Clever Clare
or Brainy Brian swagger off with the
prize while he sat prize-less at the back.
It was so unfair!

'What's the prize?' shouted Moody
Margaret.

Probably something awful like a
pencil case, thought Horrid Henry. Or
a bumper pack of school tea towels.

'Sweets!' shouted Greedy Graham.

'A million pounds!' shouted Rude
Ralph.

'Clothes!' shouted Gorgeous
Gurinder.

'A skateboard!' shouted Aerobic Al.

'A hamster!' said Anxious Andrew.

'Silence!' bellowed Miss Battle-Axe. 'The prize is a family ticket to a brand new theme park.'

Horrid Henry sat up. A theme park! Oh wow! He loved theme parks! Rollercoasters! Water rides! Candy floss! His mean, horrible parents never took him to theme parks. They dragged him to museums. They hauled him on hikes. But if he won the competition, they'd have to take him. He had to win that prize. He had to. But how could he win a

reading competition without reading
any books?

'Do comics count?' shouted Rude
Ralph.

Horrid Henry's heart leapt. He was
king of the comic book readers. He'd
easily win a comic book competition.

Miss Battle-Axe glared at Ralph
with her beady eyes.

'Of course not!' she said. 'Clare!
How many books do you think you
can read?'

'Fifteen,' said Clever Clare.

'Brian?'

'Eighteen,' said Brainy Brian.

'Nineteen,' said Clare.

'Twenty,' said Brian.

Horrid Henry smiled. Wouldn't they
get a shock when *he* won the prize? He'd
start reading the second he got home.

★

Horrid Henry stretched out in the
comfy black chair and switched on the
TV. He had plenty of time to read.
He'd start tomorrow.

Tuesday. Oh boy! Five new comics!
He'd read them first and start on all
those books later.

Wednesday. Whoopee! A Mutant
Max TV special! He'd definitely get
reading afterwards.

Thursday. Rude Ralph brought
round his great new computer game,

'Mash 'em! Smash 'em!' Henry mashed and smashed and mashed and smashed. . .

Friday. Yawn. Horrid Henry was exhausted after his long, hard week. I'll read tons of books tomorrow, thought Henry. After all, there was loads of time till the competition ended.

'How many books have *you* read, Henry?' asked Perfect Peter, looking up from the sofa.

'Loads,' lied Henry.

'I've read five,' said Perfect Peter proudly. 'More than anyone in my class.'

'Goody for you,' said Henry.

'You're just jealous,' said Peter.

'As if I'd ever be jealous of you, worm,' sneered Henry. He wandered over to the sofa. 'So what are you reading?'

'*The Happy Nappy*,' said Peter.

The Happy Nappy! Trust Peter to
read a stupid book like that.

'What's it about?' asked Henry,
snorting.

'It's great,' said Peter. 'It's all
about this nappy—' Then he
stopped. 'Wait, I'm not telling *you*.
You just want to find out so you
can use it in the competition. Well,
you're too late. Tomorrow is the
last day.'

Horrid Henry felt as if a dagger
had been plunged into his heart.
This couldn't be. Tomorrow! How
had tomorrow sneaked up so fast?

'What!' shrieked Henry. 'The
competition ends—tomorrow?'

'Yes,' said Peter. 'You should
have started reading sooner. After all,
why put off till tomorrow what you
can do today?'

'Shut up!' said Horrid Henry. He looked around wildly. What to do, what to do. He had to read something, anything—fast.

'Gimme that!' snarled Henry, snatching Peter's book. Frantically, he started to read:

'I'm unhappy, pappy,' said the snappy nappy. 'A happy nappy is a clappy—'

Perfect Peter snatched back his book.

'No!' screamed Peter, holding on tightly. 'It's mine.'

Henry lunged.

'Mine!'

'Mine!'

Riii—iippp.

'MUUUUMMMM!' screamed Peter. 'Henry tore my book!'

Mum and Dad ran into the room.

'You're fighting—over a book?' said Mum. She sat down in a chair.

'I'm speechless,' said Mum.

'Well, I'm not,' said Dad. 'Henry! Go to your room!'

'Fine!' screamed Horrid Henry.

Horrid Henry prowled up and down his bedroom. He had to think of something. Fast.

Aha! The room was full of books. He'd just copy down lots of titles. Phew. Easy-peasy.

And then suddenly Horrid Henry remembered. He had to write a book report for every book he read. Rats. Miss Battle-Axe knew loads and loads of books. She was sure to know the plot of *Jack the Kangaroo* or *The Adventures of Terry the Tea-Towel*.

Well, he'd just have to borrow Peter's list.

Horrid Henry sneaked into Peter's bedroom. There was Peter's competition entry, in the centre of Peter's immaculate desk. Henry read it.

Of course Peter would have the boring and horrible *Mouse Goes to Town*. Could he live with the shame of having baby books like *The Happy Nappy* and *Mouse Goes to Town* on his competition entry?

For a day at a theme park, anything.

Quickly, Henry copied Peter's list and book reports. Whoopee! Now he had five books. Wheel of Death here I come, thought Horrid Henry.

Then Henry had to face the terrible truth. Peter's books wouldn't be enough to win. He'd heard Clever Clare had seventeen. If only he didn't have to write those book reports. Why oh why did Miss Battle-Axe have to know every book ever written?

And then suddenly Henry had a brilliant, spectacular idea. It was so brilliant, and so simple, that Horrid

Henry was amazed. Of course there were books that Miss Battle-Axe didn't know. Books that hadn't been written—yet.

Horrid Henry grabbed his list.

'*Mouse Goes to Town*. The thrilling adventures of a mouse in town. He meets a dog, a cat, and a duck.'

Why should that poor mouse just go to town? Quickly Henry began to scribble.

'*Mouse Goes to the Country*. The thrilling adventures of a mouse in the country. He meets—'

Henry paused. What sort of things *did* you meet in the country? Henry had no idea.

Aha. Henry wrote quickly. 'He meets a sheep and a werewolf.'

'*Mouse Goes Round the World*.

80

Mouse discovers that the world is round.'

'*Mouse Goes to the Loo*. The thrilling adventures of one mouse and his potty.'

Now, perhaps, something a little different. How about *A Boy and his Pig*. What could that book be about? thought Henry.

'Once upon a time there was a boy and his pig. They played together every day. The pig went oink.'

Sounds good to me, thought Henry.

Then there was *A Pig and his Boy*.
And, of course, *A Boyish Pig. A Piggish Boy. Two Pigs and a Boy. Two Boys and a Pig*.

Horrid Henry wrote and wrote and wrote. When he had filled up four pages with books and reports, and his hand ached from writing, he stopped and counted.

Twenty-seven books! Surely that was more than enough!

★

Miss Battle-Axe rose from her seat and walked to the podium in the school hall. Horrid Henry was so excited he could scarcely breathe. He had to win. He was sure to win.

'Well done, everyone,' said Miss Battle-Axe. 'So many wonderful books read. But sadly, there can be only one winner.'

Me! thought Horrid Henry.

'The winner of the school reading competition, the winner who will be receiving a fabulous prize, is—' Horrid Henry got ready to leap up—'Clare, with twenty-eight books!'

Horrid Henry sank back down in his seat as Clever Clare swaggered up to the podium. If only he'd added *Three Boys, Two Pigs, and a Rhinoceros* to his list, he'd have tied for first. It was so unfair. All his hard work for nothing.

'Well done, Clare!' beamed Miss
Battle-Axe. She waved Clare's list. 'I see
you've read one of my very favourites,
Boudicca's Big Battle.'

She stopped. 'Oh dear. Clare, you've
put down *Boudicca's Big Battle* twice
by mistake. But never mind. I'm sure
no one else has read *twenty-seven*
books—'

'I have!' screamed Horrid Henry.
Leaping and shouting, punching the air
with his fist, Horrid Henry ran up onto
the stage, chanting: 'Theme park! Theme
park! Theme park!'

'Gimme my prize!' he screeched,
snatching the tickets out of Clare's hand.

'Mine!' screamed Clare, snatching
them back.

Miss Battle-Axe looked grim. She
scanned Henry's list.

'I am not familiar with the *Boy and Pig*

series,' she said.

'That's 'cause it's Australian,' said Horrid Henry.

Miss Battle-Axe glared at him. Then she tried to twist her face into a smile.

'It appears we have a tie,' she said.

'Therefore, you will each receive a family pass to the new theme park, Book World. Congratulations.'

Horrid Henry stopped his victory dance. Book World? Book World? Surely he'd heard wrong?

'Here are just some of the wonderful attractions you will enjoy at Book World,' said Miss Battle-Axe. ' "Thrill to a display of speed-reading! Practice checking out library books! Read to the beat!" Oh my, doesn't that sound fun!'

'AAAAAARGGGGGGGGG!' screamed Horrid Henry.

Henry's Summer Howlers

What do hedgehogs
like to eat?
Prickled onions

Why do hens watch TV?
For hentertainment.

What can you serve
but not eat?
Tennis balls.

What do you call James
Bond in the bath?
Bubble O Seven.

PERFECT PETER'S PIRATE PARTY

'Now, let's see,' said Mum, consulting her list, 'we need pirate flags, pieces of eight, swords, treasure chests, eyepatches, skull and crossbones plates. Have I missed anything?'

Horrid Henry stopped chewing. Wow! For once, Mum was talking about something important. His Purple Hand Pirate party wasn't till next month, but it was never too soon to start getting in supplies for the birthday party of the year. No, the century.

But wait. Mum had forgotten
cutlasses. They were essential for
the gigantic pirate battle Henry was
planning. And what about all the
ketchup for fake blood? And where
were the buckets of sweets?

Horrid Henry opened his mouth to
speak.

'That sounds great, Mum,' piped
Perfect Peter. 'But don't forget the
pirate napkins.'

'Napkins. Check,' said Mum, smiling.
Huh?

'I don't want napkins at my party,'
said Horrid Henry.

'This isn't for your party,' said Mum.
'It's for Peter's.'

WHAT???

'What do you mean, it's for Peter's?'
gasped Horrid Henry. He felt as if an
icy hand had gripped him by the throat.

He was having trouble breathing.

'Peter's birthday is next week, and he's having a pirate party,' said Mum.

Perfect Peter kept eating his muesli.

'But he's having a Sammy the Snail party,' said Horrid Henry, glaring at Peter.

'I changed my mind,' said Perfect Peter.

'But pirates was *my* party idea!' shrieked Horrid Henry. 'I've been planning it for months. You're just a copycat.'

'You don't own pirates,' said Peter. 'Gordon had a pirate party for his birthday. So I want pirates for mine.'

'Henry, you can still have a pirate party,' said Dad.

'NOOOOOO!' screamed Horrid Henry. He couldn't have a pirate party *after* Peter. Everyone would think he'd copied his wormy toad brother.

Henry pounced. He was a poisoned arrow whizzing towards its target.

THUD! Peter fell off his chair.

SMASH! Peter's muesli bowl crashed to the floor.

'AAAEEEIIIII!' screeched Perfect Peter. 'Look what you've done, you horrid boy!' yelled Mum. 'Say sorry to Peter.'

'WAAAAAAAAAAA!' sobbed Peter.

'I won't!' said Horrid Henry. 'I'm not sorry. He stole my party idea, and I hate him.'

'Then go to your room and stay there,' said Dad.

'It's not fair!' wailed Horrid Henry.

'What shall we do with the drunken sailor? What shall we do with the drunken sailor?' sang Perfect Peter as he walked past Henry's slammed bedroom door.

'Make him walk the plank!' screamed Horrid Henry. 'Which is what will happen to you if you don't SHUT UP!'

'Muum! Henry told me to shut up,' yelled Peter.

'Henry! Leave your brother alone,' said Mum.

'You're the eldest. Can't you be grown-up for once and let him have his party in peace?' said Dad.

NO! thought Horrid Henry. He could not. He had to stop Peter having a pirate party. He just had to.

But how?

He could bribe Peter. But that would cost money that Henry didn't have. He could promise to be nice to him . . . No way. That was going too far. That little copycat worm did not deserve Henry's niceness.

Maybe he could trick him into abandoning his party idea. Hmmmm. Henry smiled. Hmmmmm.

Horrid Henry opened Peter's bedroom door and sauntered in. Perfect Peter was busy writing names on his YO HO HO pirate invitations. The same ones, Henry noticed, that

he'd been planning to send, with the peg-legged pirate swirling his cutlass and looking like he was about to leap out at you.

'You're supposed to be in your room,' said Peter. 'I'm telling on you.'

'You know, Peter, I'm glad you're having a pirate party,' said Henry.

Peter paused.

'You are?' said Peter cautiously.

'Yeah,' said Horrid Henry. 'It means you'll get the pirate cannibal curse and I won't.'

'There's no such thing as a pirate

cannibal curse,' said Peter.

'Fine,' said Horrid Henry. 'Just
don't blame me when you end up
as a shrunken head dangling round a
cannibal's neck.'

Henry's such a liar, thought Peter.
He's just trying to scare me.

'Gordon had a pirate party, and he
didn't turn into a shrunken head,' said
Peter.

Henry sighed.

'Of course not, because his name
doesn't start with P. The cannibal pirate
who made the curse was named Blood
Boil Bob. Look, that's him on the
invitations,' said Henry.

Peter glanced at the pirate. Was it his
imagination, or did Blood Boil Bob
have an especially mean and hungry
look? Peter put down his crayon.

'He had a hateful younger brother

named Paul, who became Blood Boil
Bob's first shrunken head,' said Henry.
'Since then, the cannibal curse has
passed down to anyone else whose name
starts with P.'

'I don't believe you, Henry,' said
Peter. He was sure Henry was trying to
trick him. Lots of his friends had had

pirate parties, and none of them had
turned into a shrunken head.

On the other hand, none of his
friends had names that began with P.

'How does the curse happen?' said
Peter slowly.

Horrid Henry looked around. Then,
putting a finger to his lips, he crept over
to Peter's wardrobe and flung it open.
Peter jumped.

'Just checking Blood Boil Bob's not
in there,' whispered Henry. 'Now keep
your voice down. Remember, dressing
up as pirates, singing pirate songs,
talking about treasure, wakes up the
pirate cannibal. Sometimes — if you're
lucky — he just steals all the treasure.
Other times he . . . POUNCES,'
shrieked Henry.

Peter turned pale.

'Yo ho, yo ho, a pirate's life for me,'

sang Horrid Henry. 'Yo ho — whoops, sorry, better not sing, in case *he* turns up.'

'MUUUMMM!' wailed Peter. 'Henry's trying to scare me!'

'What's going on?' said Mum.

'Henry said I'm going to turn into a shrunken head if I have a pirate party.'

'Henry, don't be horrid,' said Mum, glaring. 'Peter, there's no such thing.'

'Told you, Henry,' said Perfect Peter.

'If I were you I'd have a Sammy the Slug party,' said Horrid Henry.

'Sammy the *Snail*,' said Peter. 'I'm having a pirate party and you can't stop me. So there.'

Rats, thought Horrid Henry. How could he make Peter change his mind?

★

101

'Don't **doooooo IT**, Peter,' Henry
howled spookily under Peter's door
every night. 'Beware! Beware!'

'Stop it, Henry!' screamed Peter.

'You'll be sorry,' Horrid Henry
scrawled all over Peter's homework.

'Remember the cannibal curse,'
Henry whispered over supper the night
before the party.

'Henry, leave your brother alone or
you won't be coming to the party,' said
Mum.

What? Miss out on chocolate pieces

of eight? Henry scowled. That was the least he was owed.

It was so unfair. Why did Peter have to wreck everything?

It was Peter's birthday party. Mum and Dad hung two huge skull and crossbones pirate flags outside the house. The exact ones, Horrid Henry noted bitterly, that he had planned for *his* birthday party. The cutlasses had been decorated and the galleon cake eaten. All that remained was for Peter's horrible guests, Tidy Ted, Spotless Sam, Goody-Goody Gordon, Perky Parveen, Helpful Hari, Tell-Tale Tim and Mini Minnie to go on the treasure hunt.

'Yo ho, yo ho, a pirate's life for me,' sang Horrid Henry. He was wearing his pirate skull scarf, his eyepatch, and his huge black skull and crossbones hat.

His bloody cutlass gleamed.

'Don't sing that,' said Peter.

'Why not, baby?' said Henry.

'You know why,' muttered Peter.

'I warned you about Blood Boil Bob, but you wouldn't listen,' hissed Henry, 'and now—' he drew his hand across his throat. 'Hey everyone, let's play pin the tail on Peter.'

'MUUUUUUUUMMMMMM!' wailed Peter.

'Behave yourself, Henry,' muttered Mum, 'or you won't be coming on the treasure hunt.'

Henry scowled. The only reason he was even at this baby party was because the treasure chest was filled with chocolate pieces of eight.

Mum clapped her hands.

'Come on everyone, look for the clues hidden around the house to help you find the pirate treasure,' she said, handing Peter a scroll. 'Here's the first one.'

Climb the stair,
if you dare,
you'll find a clue,
just for you.

'I found a clue,' squealed Helpful Hari, grabbing the scroll dangling from the banister.

> *'Turn to the left,*
> *turn to the right,*
> *reach into the bag,*
> *don't get a fright.'*

The party pounded off to the left, then to the right, where another scroll hung in a pouch from Peter's doorknob.

'I found the treasure map!' shouted Perky Parveen.

'Oh goody,' said Goody-Goody Gordon.

Everyone gathered round the ancient scroll.

'It says to go to the park,' squealed Spotless Sam. 'Look, X marks the spot where the treasure is buried.'

Dad, waving a skull and crossbones

flag, led the pirates out of the door and down the road to the park.

Horrid Henry ran ahead through the park gates and took off his skull and crossbones hat and eyepatch. No way did he want anyone to think he was part of this *baby* pirate party. He glanced at the swings. Was there anyone here that he knew? Phew, no one, just some little girl on the slide.

The little girl looked up and stared at Horrid Henry. Horrid Henry stared back.

Uh oh.

Oh no.

Henry began to back away. But it was too late.

'Henwy!' squealed the little girl. 'Henwy!'

It was Lisping Lily, New Nick's horrible sister. Henry had met her on the world's worst sleepover at Nick's house, where she—where she—

'Henwy! I love you, Henwy!' squealed Lisping Lily, running towards him. 'Will you marry with me, Henwy?'

Horrid Henry turned and ran down the windy path into the gardens. Lisping Lily ran after him. 'Henwy! Henwy!'

Henry dived into some thick bushes

and crouched behind them.

Please don't find me, please don't find me, he prayed.

Henry waited, his heart pounding. All he could hear was Peter's pirate party, advancing his way. Had he lost her?

'I think the treasure's over there!' shouted Peter.

Phew. He'd ditched her. He was safe.

'Henwy?' came a little voice. 'Henwy! Where are you? I want to give you a big kiss.'

AAAARRRGGHH!

Then Horrid Henry remembered
who he was. The boy who'd got Miss
Battle-Axe sent to the head. The boy
who'd defeated the demon dinner lady.
The boy who was scared of nothing
(except injections). What was a pirate
king like him doing hiding from some
tiddly toddler?

Horrid Henry put on his pirate hat
and grabbed his cutlass. He'd scare her
off if it was the last thing he did.

'AAAAARRRRRRRRRRR!'
roared the pirate king, leaping up and
brandishing his bloody cutlass.

'AAAAAAAAAAAHHH!' squealed
Lisping Lily. She turned and ran,
crashing into Peter.

'Piwates! Piwates!' she screamed,
dashing away.

Perfect Peter's blood ran cold. He looked

into the thrashing bushes and saw a
skull and crossbones rising out of the
hedge, the gleam of sunlight on a
blood-red cutlass…

'AAAAAAAHHHHHH!' screamed
Peter. 'It's Blood Boil Bob!' He turned
and ran.

'AAAAAAAHHHHHH!' shrieked
Ted. He turned and ran.

'AAAAAAAHHHHHH!' shrieked
Gordon, Parveen, and the rest. They
turned and ran.

Huh? thought Horrid Henry, trying to wriggle free.

Thud.

Henry's foot knocked against something hard. There, hidden beneath some leaves under the hedge, was a pirate chest.

Eureka!

★

'Help!' shrieked Perfect Peter. 'Help!
Help!'

Mum and Dad ran over.

'What's happened?'

'We got attacked by pirates!' wailed
Parveen.

'We ran for our lives!' wailed
Gordon.

'Pirates?' said Mum.

'Pirates?' said Dad. 'How many
were there?'

'Five!'

'Ten!'

'Hundreds!' wailed Mini Minnie.

'Don't be silly,' said Mum.

'I'm sure they're gone now, so let's
find the treasure,' said Dad.

Peter opened the map and headed
for the hedge nearest to the gate where
the treasure map showed a giant X.

'I'm too scared,' he whimpered.

Helpful Hari crept to the treasure chest and lifted the lid. Everyone gasped. All that was left inside were a few crumpled gold wrappers.

'The treasure's gone,' whispered Peter.

Just then Horrid Henry sauntered along the path, twirling his hat.

'Where have you been?' said Mum.

'Hiding,' said Horrid Henry truthfully.

'We got raided,' gasped Ted.

'By pirates,' gasped Gordon.

'No way,' said Horrid Henry.

'They stole all the pieces of eight,' wailed Peter.

Horrid Henry sighed.

'What did I tell you about the cannibal curse?' he said. 'Just be glad you've still got your heads.'

Hmmmm, boy, chocolate pieces of eight were always yummy, but raided pieces of eight tasted even better, thought Horrid Henry that night, shoving a few more chocolates into his mouth.

Come to think of it, there'd been too many pirate parties recently.

Now, a cannibal curse party . . . Hmmmn.

Henry's Summer Howlers

What does a dentist do
on a roller coaster?
He braces himself.

Did you hear about the
goalie with the piggy bank?
He was always saving.

What's purple and leaps from a tree?
A squirrel.
Why is it purple?
Because it choked on a nut.

Why was the skeleton
afraid of the dog?
Because dogs like bones!

Henry's Summer Howlers

What kind of
crisps can fly?
Plane.

What do you call
a woman with two
toilets on her head?
Lulu

What did one wall say to the
other wall?
Meet you at the corner.

What do you
call a computer
superhero?
A screen saver.

HORRID HENRY ROCKS

'Boys, I have a very special treat for you,' said Mum, beaming.

Horrid Henry looked up from his *Mutant Max* comic.

Perfect Peter looked up from his spelling homework.

A treat? A special treat? A very special treat? Maybe Mum and Dad were finally appreciating him. Maybe they'd got tickets . . . maybe they'd actually got tickets . . . Horrid Henry's heart leapt. Could it be possible that at last, at long last, he'd get to go to a Killer Boy Rats concert?

'We're going to the Daffy and her Dancing Daisies show!' said Mum. 'I got the last four tickets.'

'OOOOOOHHHH,' said Peter, clapping his hands. 'Yippee! I love Daffy.'

What?? NOOOOOOOOOOOO! That wasn't a treat. That was torture. A treat would be a day at the Frosty Freeze Ice Cream Factory. A treat would be no school. A treat would be all he could eat at Gobble and Go.

'I don't want to see that stupid Daffy,' said Horrid Henry. 'I want to see the Killer Boy Rats.'

'No way,' said Mum.

'I don't like the Killer Boy Rats,' shuddered Peter. 'Too scary.'

'Me neither,' shuddered Mum. 'Too loud.'

'Me neither,' shuddered Dad. 'Too shouty.'

'NOOOOOOOO!' screamed Henry.

'But Henry,' said Peter, 'everyone loves Daffy.'

'Not me,' snarled Henry.

Perfect Peter waved a leaflet. 'Daffy's going to be the greatest show ever. Read this.'

Daffy sings and dances her way across the stage and into your heart. Your chance to sing-along to all your favourite daisy songs! I'm a Lazy Daisy. Whoops-a-Daisy. And of course, Upsy-Daisy, Crazy Daisy, Prance and Dance-a-Daisy.

*

With special guest star Busy Lizzie!!!

AAAAARRRRRGGGGGGHHHHHH.

Moody Margaret's parents were taking her to the Killer Boy Rats concert. Rude Ralph was going to the Killer Boy Rats concert. Even Anxious Andrew was going, and he didn't even like them. Stuck-Up Steve had been bragging for months that he was going and would be sitting in a special box. It was so unfair.

No one was a bigger Rats fan than Horrid Henry. Henry had all their albums: Killer Boy Rats Attack-Tack-Tack, Killer Boy Rats Splat! Killer Boy Rats Manic Panic. 'It's not fair!' screamed Horrid Henry. 'I want to see the Killers!!!!'

'We have to see
something that
everyone in the family
will like,' said Mum.
'Peter's too young for the
Killer Boy Rats but we can all
enjoy Daffy.'

'Not me!' screamed Henry.

Oh, why did he have such a
stupid nappy baby for a brother?
Younger brothers should be
banned. They just wrecked
everything. When he was King
Henry the Horrible, all younger
brothers would be arrested and
dumped in a volcano.

In fact, why wait?

Horrid Henry pounced. He
was a fiery god scooping up a
human sacrifice and hurling him
into the volcano's molten depths.

'AAAIIIIIEEEEEEE!' screamed
Perfect Peter. 'Henry attacked me.'

'Stop being horrid, Henry!' shouted
Mum. 'Leave your brother alone.'

'I won't go to Daffy,' yelled Henry.
'And you can't make me.'

'Go to your room,' said Dad.

Horrid Henry paced up and down his
bedroom, singing his favourite Rats
song at the top of his lungs:

I'M DEAD, YOU'RE DEAD, WE'RE DEAD.
GET OVER IT.
DEAD IS GREAT, DEAD'S WHERE IT'S AT
'CAUSE . . .

'Henry! Be quiet!' screamed Dad.

'I am being quiet!' bellowed Henry.
Honestly. Now, how could he get
out of going to that terrible Daffy
concert? He'd easily be the oldest
one there. Only stupid babies liked
Daffy. If the horrible songs didn't
kill him then he was sure to die of
embarrassment. Then they'd be sorry
they'd made him go. But it would
be too late. Mum and Dad and Peter
could sob and boo hoo all they liked
but he'd still be dead. And serve them
right for being so mean to him.

Dad said if he was good he could
see the Killer Boys next time they
were in town. Ha. The Killer Boy
Rats NEVER gave concerts. Next
time they did he'd be old and
hobbling and whacking Peter with
his cane.

He had to get a Killer Boys ticket now. He just had to. But how? They'd been sold out for weeks.

Maybe he could place an ad:

Can you help?

Deserving Boy suffering from rare and terrible illness. His ears are falling off. Doctor has prescribed the Killer Boy Rats cure. Only by hearing the Rats live is there any hope. If you've got a ticket to the concert on Saturday PLEASE send it to Henry NOW.

(If you don't you know you'll be sorry.)

That might work. Or he could tell
people that the concert was cursed and
anyone who went would turn into a rat.
Hmmm. Somehow Henry didn't see
Margaret falling for that. Too bad Peter
didn't have a ticket, thought Henry
sadly, he could tell him he'd turn into
a killer and Peter would hand over the
ticket instantly.

And then suddenly Horrid Henry
had a brilliant, spectacular idea. There
must be someone out there who was
desperate for a Daffy ticket. In fact there
must be someone out there who would
swap a Killers ticket for a Daffy one. It
was certainly worth a try.

'Hey, Brian, I hear you've got a Killer
Boy Rats ticket,' said Horrid Henry at
school the next day.

'So?' said Brainy Brian.

'I've got a ticket to something much
better,' said Henry.

'What?' said Brian. 'The Killers are
the best.'

Horrid Henry could barely force
the grisly words out of his mouth. He
twisted his lips into a smile.

'Daffy and her Dancing Daisies,' said
Horrid Henry.

Brainy Brian stared at him.

'Daffy and her Dancing Daisies?' he spluttered.

'Yes,' said Horrid Henry brightly. 'I've heard it's their best show ever. Great new songs. You'd love it. Wanna swap?'

Brainy Brian stared at him as if he had a turnip instead of a head.

'You're trying to swap Daffy and her Dancing Daisies tickets for the Killer Boy Rats?' said Brian slowly.

'I'm doing you a favour, no one likes the Killer Boy Rats any more,' said Henry.

'I do,' said Brian.

Rats.

'How come you have a ticket for Daffy?' said Brian. 'Isn't that a baby show?'

'It's not mine, I found it,' said Horrid Henry quickly. Oops.

'Ha ha Henry, I'm seeing the Killers, and you're not,' Margaret taunted.

'Yeah Henry,' said Sour Susan.

'I heard . . .' Margaret doubled over laughing, 'I heard you were going to the Daffy show!'

'That's a big fat lie,' said Henry hotly. 'I wouldn't be seen dead there.'

Horrid Henry looked around the auditorium at the sea of little baby

nappy faces. There was Needy Neil
clutching his mother's hand. There
was Weepy William, crying because
he'd dropped his ice cream. There was
Toddler Tom, up past his bedtime.
Oh, no! There was Lisping Lily. Henry
ducked.

Phew. She hadn't seen him. Margaret
would never stop teasing him if she ever
found out. When he was king, Daffy
and her Dancing Daisies would live in
a dungeon with only rats for company.
Anyone who so much as mentioned
the name Daffy, or even grew a daisy,
would be flushed down the toilet.

There was a round of polite applause
as Daffy and her Dancing Daisies
pirouetted on stage. Horrid Henry
slumped in his seat as far as he could
slump and pulled his cap over his face.
Thank goodness he'd come disguised

and brought some earplugs. No one
would ever know he'd been.

'Tra la la la la la la!' trilled the Daisies.
'Tra la la la la la la!' trilled the
audience.

Oh, the torture, groaned Horrid
Henry as horrible song followed
horrible song. Perfect Peter sang along.
So did Mum and Dad.

AAARRRRRGGGHHHHH.

And to think that tomorrow night the Killer Boy Rats would be performing . . . and he wouldn't be there! It was so unfair.

Then Daffy cartwheeled to the front of the stage. One of the daisies stood beside her holding a giant hat.

'And now the moment all you Daffy Daisy fans have been waiting for,' squealed Daffy. 'It's the Lucky Ducky Daisy Draw, when we call up on stage an oh-so-lucky audience member to lead us in the Whoops-a-Daisy sing-a-long song! Who's it going to be?'

'Me!' squealed Peter. Mum squeezed his arm.

Daffy fumbled in the hat and pulled out a ticket.

'And the lucky winner of our ticket raffle is . . . Henry! Ticket 597! Ticket 597, yes Henry, you in row P, seat 10, come on up! Daffy needs you on stage!'

Horrid Henry was stuck to his seat in horror. It must be some other Henry. Never in his worst nightmares had he ever imagined—

'Henry, that's you,' said Perfect Peter. 'You're so lucky.'

'Henry! Come on up, Henry!' shrieked Daffy. 'Don't be shy!'

On stage at the Daffy show? No!

No! Wait till Moody Margaret found out. Wait till anyone found out. Henry would never hear the end of it. He wasn't moving. Pigs would fly before he budged.

'Henwy!' squealed Lisping Lily behind him. 'Henwy! I want to give you a big kiss, Henwy . . .'

Horrid Henry leapt out of his seat. Lily! Lisping Lily! That fiend in toddler's clothing would stop at nothing to get hold of him.

Before Henry knew what had happened, ushers dressed as daisies had nabbed him and pushed him on stage.

Horrid Henry blinked in the lights. Was anyone in the world as unlucky as he?

'All together now, everyone get ready to ruffle their petals. Let's sing Tippy-toe daisy do / Let us sing a song for you!' beamed Daffy. 'Henry, you start us off.'

Horrid Henry stared at the vast audience. Everyone was looking at him. Of course he didn't know any stupid Daisy songs. He always blocked his ears or ran from the room whenever Peter sang them. Whatever could the words be . . . 'Watch out, whoop-di-do / Daisy's doing a big poo?'

These poor stupid kids. If only they could hear some decent songs, like . . .

like . . .

'GRANNY ON HER CRUTCHES
PUSH HER OFF HER CHAIR
SHOVE SHOVE SHOVE SHOVE
SHOVE HER DOWN THE STAIRS.'

shrieked Horrid Henry.

The audience was silent. Daffy looked stunned.

'Uh, Henry . . . that's not Tippy-toe daisy do,' whispered Daffy.

'C'mon everyone, join in with me,' shouted Horrid Henry, spinning round and twirling in his best Killer Boy Rats manner.

'I'M IN MY COFFIN
NO TIME FOR COUGHIN'
WHEN YOU'RE SQUISHED DOWN DEAD.
DON'T CARE IF YOU'RE A BOFFIN
DON'T CARE IF YOU'RE A LOONY,
DON'T CARE IF YOU'RE CARTOONY
I'LL SQUISH YOU!'

sang Horrid Henry as loud as he could.

'GONNA BE A ROCK STAR (AND YOU AIN'T)
DON'T EVEN—'

Two security guards ran on stage and grabbed Horrid Henry.

'Killer Boy Rats forever!' shrieked Henry, as he was dragged off.

*

Horrid Henry stared at the special delivery letter covered in skulls and crossbones. His hand shook.

 Hey Henry,

We saw a video of you singing our songs and getting yanked off stage—way to go, killer boy! Here's a pair of tickets for our concert tonight, and a backstage pass— see you there.

 The Killer Boy Rats

139

Horrid Henry goggled at the tickets and the backstage pass. He couldn't move. He couldn't breathe. He was going to the Killer Boy Rats concert. He was actually going to the Killer Boy Rats concert.

Life, thought Horrid Henry, beaming, was sweet.

Henry's Summer Howlers

Why did the germ cross the
microscope?
To get to the other slide.

How do you make an
octopus laugh?
Ten tickles.

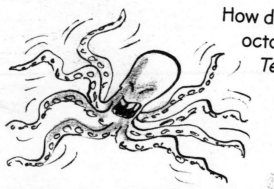

What's the best birthday
present in the world?
*A broken drum, you
can't beat it!*

Why did the chicken
carry an umbrella?
The weather was foul.

Henry's Summer Howlers

What's the worst
vegetable to
have on boat?
A leek.

Why did the girl study
on the airplane?
*She wanted a higher
education.*

Why was the girl named Sugar?
Because she was so refined.

What card game do
crocodiles play?
Snap!

Horrid Henry's Summer Boredom Busters!

Turn the page for activities, games and fun!

(Answers at the back of the book.)

Summer Countdown!

JANUARY
BRRR. It's freezing!

What's an ig?

A snow house
with no loo.

FEBRUARY

It's Henry's Birthday!

What does a snail do
on its birthday?

It shellebrates!

MARCH

Yuck, summer is still months away!

Why was the amphibian
waiting for the bus?

Because his car got
toad away!

APRIL
Getting closer . . .

When can you see
monkeys falling
from the sky?

During Ape-ril
showers.

MAY

Nearly there now . . .

What's a trampoline's
favourite time of year?

Spring!

JUNE
So close you can almost smell it . . .

When should you go at
red but stop at green?

When you're eating a
watermelon!

JULY
Summer is finally here!

What do you call witches
at the beach?

Sand-witches!

HORRID HENRY'S SUMMER GAMES

Summer is the perfect time to do nothing
except watch TV all day long, but if
you get tired of that, try one of
these fun summer games.

Who Can Blow the Loudest Trumpet?

Moody Margaret believes she'll be
the best – until she finds out that
the trumpet is a blade of grass!

You will need:

A wide blade of grass

Instructions:

1. Rinse your blade of grass with water to make sure it's clean.

2. With your fingernail, make a hole down the middle of the grass.

3. Put your thumbs on either side of the grass and press them together – so there's a small gap between your thumbs and the grass is stretched tightly in-between them.

4. Take a big breath and blow in-between your thumbs. The grass vibrates … and makes a loud noise like a trumpet. The loudest wins!

Chilly T-Shirts

A team race to pull on t-shirts – to be
played outside on a hot, sunny day!

You will need:

Two teams

One t-shirt for each
team member

A Freezer

Plastic bags

Instructions:

1. Soak all the t-shirts in water,
   then squeeze out as much
   water as you can.

2. Put each t-shirt in a separate
   plastic bag and put them all in
   the freezer overnight.

3. When you're ready to play,
   take the t-shirts out of the
   freezer.

4. Shout: Ready, Steady, Go!
   And the race is on for each
   team to defrost and pull on all
   their t-shirts.

HOLIDAY HIGHLIGHTS

Horrid Henry's family, friends, and
enemies have special holiday highlights.
Untangle the names and work out
who enjoyed what.

1. Day out at a theme park   EAATGRMR

Answer: __ __ __ __ __ __ __ __

2. Watching a football match   SMSI ELBTTA-XEA

Answer: __ __ __ __   __ __ __ __ __ __ - __ __ __

3. Swimming with dolphins   GGSYO DSI

Answer: __ __ __ __ __   __ __ __

4. Long lie-ins every day   DNLIA

Answer: __ __ __ __ __

5. Trip to an ice cream factory   MGAAHR

Answer: __ __ __ __ __ __

6. Going on a nature trail   RPTEE

Answer: __ __ __ __ __

7. Attending the Summer School
for Clever Kids   NBRAI and EALCR

Answer: __ __ __ __ __
and   __ __ __ __ __

CAR GAMES

Horrid Henry HATES long car journeys. Make them more fun by looking out the window and trying to spot something beginning with every letter of Henry's FAVOURITE holiday treat.

C_____

H_____

O_____

C_____

O_____

L_____

A_____

T_____

E_____

Now can you find something beginning with every letter of one of Horrid Henry's LEAST favourtie foods?

M_____

U_____

E_____

S_____

L_____

I_____

SLIMY SLIME

Rude Ralph and Horrid Henry have a secret recipe for their super-gross out slimy slime. Learn how to make it below!

You will need:

Water

A measuring jug

A saucepan

Green food colouring

Unflavoured gelatine (3 sachets)

Golden syrup

A fork

A small plastic container with a lid

A dessert spoon

Instructions:

1. Measure 2fl oz of water and pour it into the pan.

2. Ask an adult to heat up the water until it boils, and then take it off the heat.

3. Add a tiny drop of green food colouring to the water.

4. Sprinkle in three sachets of gelatine.

5. Leave the gelatine to soften for 2–3 minutes, then stir with a fork.

6. Add two dessertspoons of golden syrup.

7. Stir with a fork and lift out the long slimy strands of green goo.

8. As it cools, you'll need to add more water, a little at a time until it is nice and gooey.

9. To give your slime as a present, pop it into a plastic container and put the lid on tightly!

TV RULES, READING DROOLS

There's nothing worse than parents banning you from watching TV during your summer holidays! If they try to make you read instead, use Horrid Henry's list of 10 reasons TV is better than reading.

1. Holding a book is very tiring.

2. Turning pages is very tiring.

3. Moving your eyes from left to right is very tiring.

4. You can eat crisps while watching TV.

5. You can chat while watching TV.

6. You can do your homework while watching TV.

7. You can play computer games and watch TV at the same time.

8. You can dance while watching TV.

9. There are great programmes on TV, like *Hog House* and *Knight Fight* and *Terminator Gladiator*.

10. No one ever tests you about what you watched on TV.

HORRIBLE H WORDS

How many words can you think
of that start with the letter H?
Bonus points for words over 5 letters!

_____   _____

_____   _____

_____   _____

_____   _____

_____   _____

_____   _____

_____   _____

_____   _____

_____   _____

_____   _____

WORD MUDDLE

How many words can you make using
only the letters from one of Horrid Henry's
favourite nicknames for Perfect Peter?

SMELLY NAPPY BABY

_____   _____

_____   _____

_____   _____

_____   _____

_____   _____

_____   _____

_____   _____

_____   _____

_____   _____

SECRET CODE

Horrid Henry has written a note to Perfect
Peter. He's used a secret code so that his
mum and dad won't read it and stop him
watching TV. Can you break the code
and read the note?

CLUE: If A = Z and Z = A,
can you work out all the letters in between?

Now use Horrid Henry's code to write
your own note to Perfect Peter.

WHAT'S IN THE BOX?

Cross out all the letters that appear more than three times on Horrid Henry's box. Then rearrange the five letters that are left to find out what's inside.

Write your answer here: _ _ _ _ _ KIT

GETTING FROM A–Z

Can you change the first word to
the last word by only changing one
letter at a time? Each word in the
middle has to be a real word!

FISH
———————

———————

———————

———————

———————

CAKE
———————

HORRID HENRY'S TOUGH TEST

The best thing about summer is more
time for the Purple Hand Gang – but
if you want to join you'll have to
prove you have what it takes!

1. **Which of these is the best club rule?**
    a. No girls allowed!
    b. No boys allowed!
    c. Do a good deed every day.

2. **What's your favourite plan to attack a rival gang?**
    a. Raid their biscuit tin and stinkbomb their den.
    b. Set a booby trap and soak them all!
    c. Let's all be friends and play nicely.

3. **Choose your top two Stinky Stinkbomb ingredients?**
    a. Dead fish and rotten eggs.
    b. Boys' smelly socks and dog poo.
    c. Mummy's perfume and pretty flowers.

4. **Which activities are the most fun?**
   a. Scoffing biscuits and beating the girls' gang.
   b. Writing secret messages and spying on the boys' gang.
   c. Doing good deeds and keeping the den neat and tidy.

5. **What's your favourite stash of club grub?**
   a. Chocolate biscuits pinched from the girls' den – he he!
   b. Chocolate fudge chewies sneaked from the boys' den – nah nah ne nah nah!
   c. Carrot sticks and apples – so healthy and delicious.

6. **How would you choose your club members?**
   a. They need a special skill, like burping – or bring plenty of sweets and other club grub.
   b. They have to obey the leader at all times.
   c. They should be tidy, spotless and well-behaved.

7. **What's the best sort of leader?**

   a.   Brave, clever, amazing.

   b.   Bossy, grouchy, mean.

   c.   Good, kind, helpful.

8. **A club member has been caught spying for the rival gang. What's the best punishment?**

   a.   Banishment for ever.

   b.   Never speaking to the sneaky spy again.

   c.   Hold a club meeting, and ask the spy to hand in their membership book and badge, and leave quietly.

SEASIDE SUDOKUS

Can you solve these seaside sudokus?
Every coloured box must contain one shell,
one starfish, one sun and one ice cream.

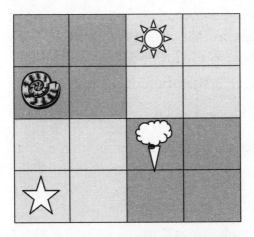

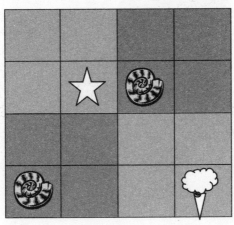

MAKE A PIRATE HAT

Have your own pirate party with these
pirate hats made from newspaper.

You will need:

A piece of paper

Tape

Pens, crayons or paint

Glue

1.

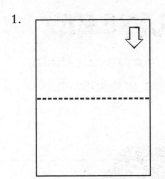

Instructions:

1. Fold the piece of paper in half.

2. Fold in the top corners to make a triangle, leaving a small strip at the bottom.

3. Fold up the bottom strip, then turn over and fold up the strip on the other side.

4. Tape the sides to make the hat stronger.

5. Draw or paint a skull and crossbones on the white paper. Cut it out and stick it onto the front of the hat.

2.

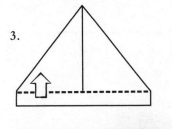

3.

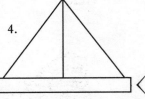

4.

5.

DELICIOUS TREATS

Fizzywizz! Ice pops! Pizza Parties! Summer is full of delicious foods. What are your top five summer treats?

1. _____

2. _____

3. _____

4. _____

5. _____

FREEDOM!

School's out but parents still have to work!
What are five things you would do if you
had the house to yourself all day?

1. _____

2. _____

3. _____

4. _____

5. _____

TOP TRICKS

Summer means plenty of time for playing tricks on your enemies. Get some ideas with Henry's list of his best ever tricks!

1. Scaring the Best Boys Club into giving me all their money by pretending there was a Fangmangler monster in the garden.

2. Telling Peter that a cardboard box was a time machine and making him think he'd travelled to the future.

3. Grabbing everyone's Halloween sweets despite being stuck at home.

4. Getting rid of Greasy Greta, the Demon Dinner Lady, by putting hot chilli powder in her biscuits.

5. Tricking Bossy Bill into photocopying his bottom.

6. Switching the present tags on Stuck-Up Steve's gifts and mine, so that I got Steve's great gifts and Steve got my horrible ones.

7. Persuading Bossy Bill and Stuck-Up Steve to wear pyjamas for a paintballing party.

8. Escaping from Moody Margaret's school by telling her mum me and Peter had been sick.

9. Terrifying Stuck-Up Steve into thinking there was a monster under his bed.

10. Showing the Bogey Babysitter who's boss by frightening her with a spider in a jar.

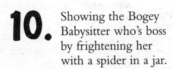

SNAIL TRAIL
TANGLED STRINGS

The Purple Hand Gang, the Secret Club
and the Best Boys are holding a snail race.
Follow the slime trails and find out which
club comes 1st, 2nd and 3rd.

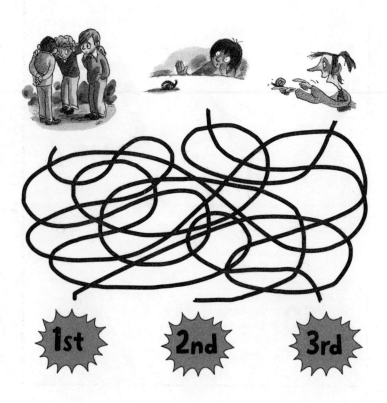

MY DREAM HOLIDAY

Horrid Henry dreams of going on holiday to Lazy Life Campsite where there is swimming, music and TV. Draw a picture of your dream holiday here.

SUMMER SUDOKU

Fill in the sudokus so that every square
and row – both up and down – contains
a picture of a tennis racket, a football,
a hockey stick and a bicycle.

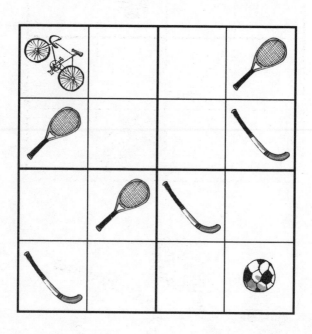

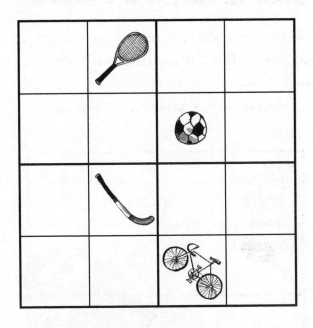

SUMMER HOWLERS

Match the punchlines below to some
of Henry's favourite jokes!

3 letters	4 letters	5 letters
moo	head	grape
	nose	smell
		boots

6 letters	8 letters
carrot	nostrils
pooper	

1. What's purple and sounds like an ape?
   A _ _ _ _ _ .

2. What do you get if you sit under a cow?
   A pat on the _ _ _ _ .

3. Why do giraffes have long necks?
   Because their feet _ _ _ _ _ .

4.   How do you catch a rabbit?
     Hide behind a tree and make a noise
     like a _ _ _ _ _ _ .

5.   Why do gorillas have big fingers?
     Because they have big

     _ _ _ _ _ _ _ _ .

6.   Why didn't the centipede get picked
     for the football team?
     It took him hours to get his
     _ _ _ _ _   on.

7.   How do you stop a skunk smelling?
     Hold his _ _ _ _ .

8.   Why did Peter take toilet paper to
     the party?
     Because he was a party

     _ _ _ _ _ _ .

9.   What do you say to a cow on its
     birthday?
     Happy birthday to _ _ _ .

STUCK-UP STEVE'S FORTUNE TELLER

Steve uses a fortune teller to predict what he and his friends are going to get for their birthdays – learn how to make one yourself below.

You will need:

A square piece of paper

Crayons, pens or colouring pencils

1.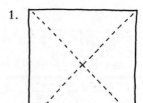

Instructions:

1. Find the middle of the paper by folding it from opposite corner to corner.

2.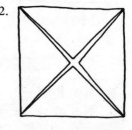

2. Fold each corner to the centre to make a smaller square.

3.

3. Turn the square over, and turn each corner to the centre again to make an even smaller square.

4.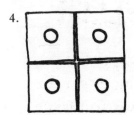

4. Turn over again. Draw a different colour on each quarter of the square.

5. Turn over again. Put a number from 1–8 on each segment.

6. Open out each flap and write a different present behind each number.

5.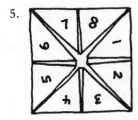

6.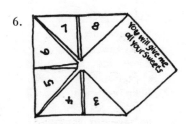

199

7.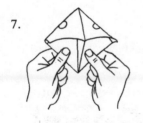

7. Put the thumb and forefinger of each hand into a segment and close up the fortune-teller. Ask your victim to choose a colour.

8.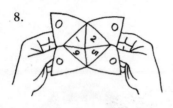

8. If they choose RED, spell out R-E-D, and open and shut the fortune-teller three times. Then ask your victim to choose a number from the four numbers showing.

9.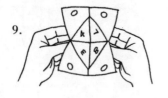

9. Open and shut the fortune-teller however many times they choose. Then finally ask them to choose another number, open up the flap and tell them which present they are going to get!

Goodbye Gang!

ANSWERS

p.162–163

p.166–167

1. Margaret
2. Miss Battle-Axe
3. Soggy Sid
4. Linda
5. Graham
6. Peter
7. Brian and Clare

p.176

The note says: Peter is smelly

p.178

Mummy

p.179

One possible answer is:
FISH
WISH
WASH
CASH
CASE
CAKE

p.180–182

1. a
2. a
3. a
4. a
5. a
6. a
7. a
8. a

If you got mostly B's, you belong in Margaret's club.
If you got mostly C's, you belong in Smelly Peter's club.

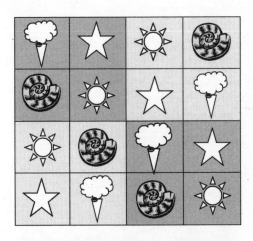

205

p.188–189

p.192

1st: Peter
2nd: Henry
3rd: Margaret

p.194

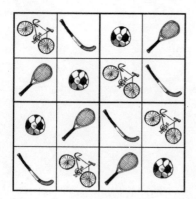

p.195

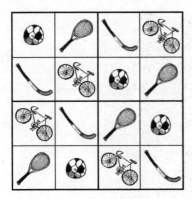

p.196–197

1. grape
2. head
3. smell
4. carrot
5. nostrils
6. boots
7. nose
8. pooper
9. moo

Storybooks

Horrid Henry
Horrid Henry and the Secret Club
Horrid Henry Tricks the Tooth Fairy
Horrid Henry's Nits
Horrid Henry Gets Rich Quick
Horrid Henry's Haunted House
Horrid Henry and the Mummy's Curse
Horrid Henry's Revenge
Horrid Henry and the Bogey Babysitter
Horrid Henry's Stinkbomb
Horrid Henry's Underpants
Horrid Henry Meets the Queen

Early Readers

Colour Books

Horrid Henry's Big Bad Book
Horrid Henry's Wicked Ways
Horrid Henry's Evil Enemies
Horrid Henry Rules the World
Horrid Henry's House of Horrors
Horrid Henry's Dreadful Deeds
Horrid Henry Shows Who's Boss
Horrid Henry's A-Z of Everything Horrid
Horrid Henry's Fearsome Four
Horrid Henry's Royal Riot
Horrid Henry's Tricky Tricks
Horrid Henry's Lucky Dip

Joke Books

Horrid Henry's Joke Book
Horrid Henry's Jolly Joke Book
Horrid Henry's Mighty Joke Book
Horrid Henry versus Moody Margaret
Horrid Henry's Hilariously Horrid Joke Book
Horrid Henry's Purple Hand Gang Joke Book
Horrid Henry's All Time Favourite Joke Book
Horrid Henry's Jumbo Joke Book

Activity Books

Horrid Henry's Brainbusters
Horrid Henry's Headscratchers
Horrid Henry's Mindbenders
Horrid Henry's Colouring Book
Horrid Henry's Puzzle Book
Horrid Henry's Sticker Book
Horrid Henry Runs Riot
Horrid Henry's Classroom Chaos
Horrid Henry's Holiday Havoc
Horrid Henry's Wicked Wordsearches
Horrid Henry's Mad Mazes
Horrid Henry's Crazy Crosswords
Horrid Henry's Big Bad Puzzle Book
Horrid Henry's Gold Medal Games
Where's Horrid Henry?
Horrid Henry's Crafty Christmas
Where's Horrid Henry Colouring Book

Fact Books

Horrid Henry's Ghosts
Horrid Henry's Dinosaurs
Horrid Henry's Sports
Horrid Henry's Food
Horrid Henry's King and Queens
Horrid Henry's Bugs
Horrid Henry's Animals
Horrid Henry's Ghosts
Horrid Henry's Crazy Creatures

Visit Horrid Henry's website at
www.horridhenry.co.uk for competitions,
games, downloads and a monthly newsletter

COMING SOON:

HORRID HENRY
GHOSTS AND GHOULS

Celebrate all things spooky with
this seriously ghoulish story collection!
Zombie vampires, were-rabbits and
things that go bump in the night –
plus games, jokes and activities
to create your own fiendishly
funny mischief.

WHERE'S HORRID HENRY?

Featuring 32 pages of things to spot, join
Henry and his friends (and evilest enemies!)
on their awesome adventures – from
birthday parties and camping trips
to hiding out at a spooky haunted house.
With a challenging checklist of things to
find, this is Henry's most horrid
challenge yet!

The question is, where's Horrid Henry?

HORRID HENRY'S CANNIBAL CURSE

The final collection of four brand new utterly horrid stories in which Horrid Henry triumphantly reveals his guide to perfect parents, reads an interesting book about a really naughty girl, and conjures up the cannibal's curse to deal with his enemies and small, annoying brother.